When Nobody's Home
Fifteen Baby-sitting Tales of Terror

Also by Judith Gorog:

When Nobody's Home

Fifteen Baby-sitting Tales of Terror

Judith Gorog

SCHOLASTIC INC.
New York Toronto London Auckland Sydney

ISBN 0-590-46874-X

12 11 10 9 8 7 6 5 4 3 2 1   8 9/9 0 1 2 3/0

Printed in the U.S.A.   01

First Scholastic paperback printing, October 1998

For the housemates at UC Berkeley,
and the Artins of Boston

Contents

When Nobody's Home

Fifteen Baby-sitting Tales of Terror

New Sitter

On Monday, right after breakfast, our mother said to us, "Miz Demay won't be coming to stay with you this Friday night."

"Lately," our father added in his most serious voice, "we hear reports that you have been a little bit out of hand." We started to defend ourselves, but Father put up his hands. "Tut, tut, tut. Not a word. Mother and I will evaluate the situation after we hear what the new sitter has to say."

In private we scoffed. Our parents would never get a new sitter. Where would they find one? They only knew Miz Demay. They could not fool us. We knew that book from when we were little kids, the one where the class is bad, and so the teacher, Miss Nelson, pretends to be missing. What really happens is that Miss Nelson dresses up in wrinkled stockings, an ugly dress, a mask, and a fright wig and comes in to the class and is so mean that the kids reform on the spot. Fine, we agreed; we could take a joke, and we could wait for Friday night.

On Tuesday and Wednesday, we searched our parents' faces for hints that they knew it really would be Miz Demay coming on Friday, but in disguise.

On Thursday we started to feel a bit edgy. Our parents were so calm, and what if there *was* a new sitter? We started asking. What's the new sitter like? Old? Or is it a guy? Or maybe it isn't a sitter. I mean, we are big enough not to have a sitter.

"You'll see." That was all Mother said, and she did have a small smile as she turned away.

Friday night came. The knocker on the front door banged. We raced to answer it, but Father held up his hand. "Tut. Tut. We'll get the door."

We waited.

Our parents opened the door, gave a brief greeting, and went out. The door closed, and there, in our front hall, stood a small young woman dressed all in black. She had on a backpack, and her black hair was covering her face 'cause she was bent over taking off these steel-tipped biker boots. I never saw how she did it. I mean, it was all one movement: She took off her boots and took off her backpack and took out some boards and, man, she broke those boards into kindling. I have never seen anything like it. The way she moved, it was like water from her hands that the boards went into the fireplace and she was over there lighting them. I never got a fire started that fast.

I admit it; I was gaping. This was not Miz Demay in a costume.

"Awesome. Is that some sort of karate?"

"No." The young woman put the screen in front of the grate. How could a voice as soft as hers sound sort of mean? "You saw something of a discipline so strict that I am forbidden even to utter its name. It requires that one spend years watching the masters and thinking, before you attempt anything with your own body. My name is Hane, and I am a housemate of your big sister at UC Berkeley. Your sister thinks I am something of an expert on baby-sitting." As she spoke, she walked over to her backpack and took out a folder, which she carried back to the fire.

She sat down on the couch and stared at the fire. "I tell you what, guys. I am so tired from finishing this book of baby-sitter stories." She tapped the folder. "I need a little shut-eye." She lay down on the couch and closed her eyes. "We can read them later, when I wake up."

She went to sleep! She wasn't kidding, either. Your eyeballs twitch when you fake. She just came to our house, and turned us loose. We could do anything we wanted. But first, I picked up the folder. We might as well take a peek.

The Snooping Sitter

Have you heard the one about the snooping baby-sitter?

That sentence, at the top of the page, demanded full attention. June bit firmly into the apple, holding it with her teeth, which left both hands free to slide the thin sheaf of papers from the pile on the desk. This job already was more interesting than most.

Adjusting the desk lamp as she settled into the chair, June read on, eating the apple carefully so that no juice splattered onto the clean white pages. The story continued, detailing the habits of the snooping baby-sitter, a girl who was, to June's mind, pretty timid in her explorations. In the story, the girl's end came rather abruptly when she opened a closet door to discover the glittering blade of a guillotine descending upon her.

June shrugged, put the story back into the pile

of papers, then continued her examination of the contents of the desk: bank statements, credit card bills. These people lived pretty high on the hog.

"Have you heard the one about the snooping baby-sitter?" June sang the words softly to herself, again and again, changing the beat each time. Funny idea, a story like that. June took one last bite of apple. Wonder if the husband or the wife wrote it?

Abandoning the desk, June set off to check out the wife's dressing room/closet, making sure to look in on the kid on the way. In his crib, the toddler, fanny up, slept soundly. As was her usual practice with a new baby-sitting job, June had put him to bed early, then waited until he was sleeping soundly before she began to poke around. Until kids learned to tell time, you could send them to bed hours before the parents specified.

To June's way of thinking, once the kids were safely asleep, it was time to explore. As usual in a new place, June had begun in the kitchen, opening cabinets and cupboards to see what the people ate, what vitamins they consumed. The food had been mostly healthy, the kitchen bare of knickknacks or appliances, except for the one serious, professional-model knife sharpener. When she had seen enough,

June turned off the light and left the kitchen.

The bathroom came next, with its storehouse of secrets: medications and evidence of private practices. One by one, June carefully, quietly, opened cabinets, but stopped when she heard sounds from outside the bathroom. Quickly, June flushed the toilet, opened the bathroom door, then walked into the hall. No one there. The sounds came from the kid's room. June tiptoed in. The child stirred, muttered in his sleep, then fell silent once again.

From the desk, June returned to the kitchen to dispose of the apple core and wash her sticky fingers. After the closets, she'd go back to the kitchen to find something else to eat. You worked up an appetite while you explored. June snooped systematically. Whenever she baby-sat, desks came after bathrooms, desks rich with their calendar notes, papers, and bills. Somewhere, maybe in the living room, maybe in the study, June always found her favorite, the first thing she had ever enjoyed while baby-sitting, the most harmless, the thing no one would ever mind her seeing. Funny, the most benign pastime, the one she still liked best of all, the simple pleasure of leafing through photo albums, had led her to further snooping, until June had become a consummate spy.

"Have you heard the one . . . about the snooping baby-sitter?" June hummed as she touched each garment.

This woman's closet wasn't much of a disappointment. After all, you could pretty much tell what would be in there once you saw what she had upon her body when she went out tonight. Dull, dull, dull; hangers and shelves full of outdated stuff. This woman must not have thrown anything away since she was seventeen.

The man's closet? Not even worth opening. June shrugged. That about finished the place. Time to return to the living room, to leaf through the photo albums once more before the people returned home. It would be time for another apple. Hmmm. Utility closet not worth opening, not to see vacuum cleaners and dust cloths. The front hall closets? Maybe they had china or silver or something worth seeing.

Locked.

No problem. June smiled. She had never seen a closet she could not open, and with never a trace.

June pulled open the narrow door, poked her head in to look for the light. From the corner of her eye, she saw the blade as it fell, not a shining blade at all. The story lied; this one was all rusty, dark with dried blood.

8

Doglicks

At the merest mention of baby-sitting, Sasha always backed away. No; no; no; and No, thank you. Sasha was not interested in taking care of children, not of wet infants, not of drooling toddlers, and not of board-game-addicted grammar schoolers. Sasha had been refusing baby-sitting jobs forever, until, finally, most people stopped asking her.

Sasha turned down baby-sitting jobs for several reasons. The one she always said aloud was that she really did not particularly like anyone younger than twenty. The real, true, secret-in-her-heart reason was that Sasha was terrified to be in someone else's house, especially as the most grown-up person in that house. And, most especially, at night. Truth was, she not only turned down baby-sitting jobs. Sasha always told other kids that she was not allowed to spend the night, not allowed to accept any sleepover invitations. Truth was, Sasha never had a peaceful minute in someone else's house once the sun went down.

Actually, Sasha grew tense the instant she went in the door of another house, when first she smelled the smells of a house not her own. After dark, she grew cold with terror at the first creak of an unfamiliar house.

Sasha, for sixteen years, stayed every night in her own bed in her own room, in her own house.

Sasha would have spent a certain weekend the very same way, if there had not been an incredibly complicated series of circumstances that finally included Sasha's very own mother begging her to take a weekend-long baby-sitting job with seven-year-old twins and their huge, friendly, affectionate, and most reassuring retriever. The dog clinched the deal. Sasha adored dogs, especially large affectionate and reassuring dogs. With the dog in the house, what could scare her? With the dog in the house, Sasha knew she could get through the weekend.

Because she could not bear to think of sitting up terrified and alone in a strange house after the twins went to sleep, even with that large and affectionate dog for companionship, Sasha planned to go to bed, to sleep, the minute the twins did.

Friday evening passed pretty well. The Thompson twins were okay kids. Sasha made popcorn; she played cards with them. They watched cartoon movies, and every so often treated themselves to stupendous pillow fights, until all of them, even the dog, were yawning big ones. Lucky for Sasha, the twins had each other for company, with no need for her to sit with them until they fell asleep.

Whew. Sasha could jump straight into the guest room bed, with that sweet dog on the floor close by. If Sasha should awake, afraid in the dark, hearing things in the night, the dog would be there. All Sasha had to do was reach out over the edge of the bed, and the dog, as if it knew how much she needed it, gave her hand a reassuring lick.

Indeed, that night Sasha did awaken once, but never let herself feel afraid. She reached out for the dog. That obliging creature awoke itself from a fine doggy dream and gave Sasha's outstretched hand a nice wet lick.

Sasha's plan for Saturday had been to take the twins for a long bicycle ride. That good idea, however, got soaked with rain, which fell hard and steady all morning. Sasha could see that it was going to be a long, long day, so right after lunch she and the twins put themselves into slickers and boots, then took the dog through every puddle in the neighborhood.

They got home sopping wet, used lots of towels to dry the retriever, then took hot showers to warm themselves. After they finished, the darned shower simply would not go completely off, but kept on drip, drip, dripping. Finally Sasha tied a towel to the showerhead to act as a wick. Although the water then ran quietly down the towel to the drain, Sasha could not relax, but still kept straining to hear. Was it quiet, or was it still drip, drip, dripping?

In that way Saturday evening dragged. Sasha tried to make the hours go quickly. They ate and played games, danced and sang to the radio and some CDs, but how slowly the hours passed! The twins seemed to be having a pretty good time, while Sasha longed for Sunday to come, for the Thompson parents to return. If only her mother could come to spend the night, or, even better, if only Sasha could take the twins and the dog home, to sleep in her very own room. But no. Sasha and her mother had been over all the possibilities. Sasha could handle this baby-sitting job. She could. Nevertheless, shortly before the twins' bedtime, Sasha telephoned her mother, whose replies were cheerful and firm. "You're doing *fine,* dear. Everything will be just *fine;* now hang up the phone and put those children to bed. The doors are locked. You are perfectly safe, and you have that nice doggie to keep you company. Night night." And Sasha's mother hung up the phone.

Sasha reached out for the dog. The dog, as if it understood, licked Sasha's outstretched fingers. Sasha scratched the dog's head, got up from her chair to hug the dog and tell it how wonderful it was. The dog thumped its tail on the floor, blinked its golden eyes.

At last it was time for bed. The twins brushed their teeth, giggled until they slept. Sasha, tense, listened to the rain, to the drip, drip, drip of water falling on the leaves outside, to the rush of water down the drain spouts. She could hear branches scraping the house. She could hear every sound that made her afraid.

With the dog walking beside her, Sasha got up and once more checked the locked doors and windows, and then returned to bed. In the dark, Sasha listened to the rain. At last, she fell asleep.

Later, in the darkest part of the night, Sasha awoke to hear the sounds of the night. The rain had stopped, but outside there was water drip, drip, dripping. And, inside, from the bathroom, came the sound of drip, drip, dripping. In the dark, Sasha swallowed, but the lump of fear in her chest did not go away. *Drip, drip, drip.* The towel must have slipped off the showerhead, Sasha reasoned, but she was too scared to get up to put it back. Timidly, Sasha reached out over the edge of the bed. That warm wet tongue on her outstretched fingers reassured her. Thinking what a very good dog it was, Sasha went back to sleep.

In the gray before dawn, Sasha awoke again to the sounds of the dripping from the bathroom. She listened to it, and to the wind whipping the leaves outside. Trembling, Sasha reached out from under the covers with her fingertips, reached for the large dog that slept there in the room on the floor beside the bed. Once again Sasha was comforted by that warm tongue. Once again Sasha was grateful for that sweet dog letting her know that everything was fine. Before long it would be morning. Before long the baby-sitting job would be over. Before long, Sasha would be back at home. Sasha knew she would miss the dog. Perhaps she could visit the dog sometimes? Sasha fell back asleep, thinking of the dog.

The glare of bright sunlight right in her eyes woke Sasha. She sat straight up in bed, wondering how could it have gotten so late. The twins were early risers. Sasha had to get going. When she looked, Sasha could see that the dog was already gone from the floor beside the bed.

As she walked to the bathroom, Sasha heard clearly the drip, drip, dripping that had disturbed her in the night. The wick towel must have gotten heavy with water, then fallen down from the show-erhead. It was too irritating. Sasha decided that before she did anything else, she simply had to put that towel back. Even with the bathroom door closed, you could hear that blasted dripping.

The door closed?

Sasha knew she had left the bathroom door open. Never mind. Maybe one of the twins was inside. Sasha knocked at the bathroom door.

Silence.

Sasha called the Thompson twins by name.

No answer.

Sasha opened the bathroom door. Sasha saw what made the dripping sound.

She saw, hanging in the shower, the bodies of the Thompson twins, the body of their large, re-assuring dog, and more.

No! said the message, written in blood on the bathroom tiles.

Know, Sasha! Not only a dog can lick your hand in the night.

A Small Child
and a Large Sitter

Caroline Louise Emily Beth, a small, frail seven-year-old, was left one night by her parents in the care of a new baby-sitter. The sitter, a strapping girl with masses of curly brown hair growing out of her head in all directions, arrived at the house on a large black bicycle.

Caroline Louise Emily Beth watched silently as the sitter wheeled the bicycle into the front hall. Caroline Louise Emily Beth stood very still while her mother, dressed all in silk, fragrant with their favorite perfume, leaned over to give the child a kiss. Her father, splendid in formal clothes, bent down, whispered his usual corny old joke in the child's ear, but Caroline Louise did not smile. She could not remove her eyes from the face of that new sitter, with its expression of scorn and something else. Hatred perhaps?

16

After the big front door closed behind the parents, the sitter said, "Dinner." The small frail child led the sitter into the kitchen, where dinner was waiting for them. Mother had made all Caroline Louise's favorite foods, which the child ate with acceptable appetite. When she had finished with her meal, the sitter pointed to the table and said, "Clear."

When Caroline had finished putting the plates and utensils into the dishwasher, the sitter said, "I will play two board games with you. No more."

"Thank you," replied the child, "but no, thank you. I'll build with Lego." She did, and by turning her back to the sitter, Caroline Louise Emily Beth passed the time rather pleasantly.

Abruptly, the sitter said, "Bedtime, Caroline."

Caroline Louise looked first at the clock, which said eight exactly, and then at the sitter, before asking politely if she might stay up just long enough to complete what she had been building.

The sitter's already grim face grew slightly red.

"Absolutely not."

Faced with such rigidity, Caroline Louise attempted, with great patience, to explain that her parents and other sitters allowed her a grace period of a few minutes to complete a project.

17

The sitter's eyes flashed. Hands on hips, she towered over the child. It was real menace in her voice when she repeated, "Bedtime."

"In my country," said the sitter, hauling the child to her feet with a fistful of Caroline's shirt, "we *strap* into their beds at night those wicked, stubborn, nasty little girls who refuse to go to bed at the time they are ordered!"

Those words, clearly intended to make the child afraid, had the desired effect. Without a sound, Caroline Louise Emily Beth stood up, put away the Lego, and walked out of the playroom.

Caroline Louise Emily Beth went to her bedroom, where she put on her pajamas, brushed her teeth, and got into her bed. There she lay, in the dark, until the sitter had come to the door, glanced inside, then gone away again. For what seemed a long time, the child lay there, eyes open, listening. At last the sounds coming from the living room indicated that the sitter had settled down on the couch that faced the television.

Slowly, Caroline Louise Emily Beth raised herself into a sitting position. There, for more than an hour, she sat on her bed, crosslegged, her hands clasped around her feet, listening. At first, the sitter clicked through the channels, watching two-three-four shows at once. Then, as she grew drowsy, the sounds coming from the TV set indicated that it had remained for some time on one channel.

Cautiously, the small, frail seven-year-old crept out of bed, down the hall, around the corner to a spot that offered an unobstructed view of the sitter on the sofa facing the television. Hands folded under her cheek, her body filling the sofa from end to end, the sitter slept.

At that sight, Caroline Louise Emily Beth smiled for the first time since the arrival of the new baby-sitter. Silently the child turned, raced down the stairs, down the hall, to the kitchen, where she paused long enough to reach into a cupboard for a glass measuring cup, into a drawer for a teaspoon. Then, quietly, she went out the back door, closing the screen carefully behind her. Within minutes, she had filled the measuring cup half full of slugs, not the giant speckled ones, but the tiny yellow ones, whose slime is the thickest, most yellow, most difficult to remove of all the slug slimes the child knew.

On tiptoe, back into the house she went, stopping in the kitchen long enough to warm the container of slugs in a basin of water. The spoon, too, she warmed to body temperature. Then, a tiny smile on her tiny face, the child crept into the living room, where the sitter slept on the sofa facing the giant television screen. Carefully, the child spooned, one at a time, five yellow slugs into the hair of the sleeping sitter. That task accomplished, Caroline Louise Emily Beth placed slugs beneath the roll of sock above the ankle of the sleeping sitter. One here, one there, a slug in a pocket, a slug under the waistband of the sitter's summer shorts. Through all of this, the sitter snored softly.

At last, with just three slugs left, the child stood up, eased the cramps in her shoulders. She walked over to the sitter's black bicycle, put a slug on each of the handlegrips. Then, after giving a last, long, and thoughtful look at the remaining slug, the child crept back to the sofa. It was risky, she had decided, but worth the try. Holding her breath, she slowly placed that last slug into the cup of the sitter's left ear. The sitter barely stirred.

The job done, the child returned the utensils to the kitchen, put them into the dishwasher.

After one good stretch, one great yawn, the child returned to her bed. She pulled the covers up to her chin, and smiling, fell instantly asleep. She slept so well and so deeply, and dreamed such pleasant dreams, that she did not hear a sound of what took place later that night. As it was, her pleasure was complete. Caroline Louise Emily Beth never saw that sitter again.

Lupe and the Forgetful Family

When my friend Lupe went to baby-sit for the forgetful family, she was dead tired, beat from working three jobs that summer. Lupe, herself, had forgotten that the family is really rich — they pay the best of anyone we baby-sit for — and she had forgotten that they are really, really strange.

Actually, Lupe took that job, tired as she was, because I, tired as I was, had goofed. I'd promised to sit for two different families that night, so Lupe went to baby-sit the Little Forgetful to help me out.

When Lupe got to the house, the forgetful father forgot to tell her that the family had a new pet, a nine-foot regal python, a mere tot as regal pythons go because that sort of snake can grow to be thirty feet long.

The forgetful mother forgot to tell Lupe that the new pet was affectionate, accustomed to taking a nap while coiled around the warm human body of one or another member of the forgetful family.

The forgetful big sister, who was going out that night with her friends, forgot to tell Lupe that the family pet was a bit of a glutton for fresh peaches, which were then plentiful, luscious, and ripe at the height of the season.

And, last of all, the small forgetful child forgot to tell Lupe or anyone else that he had accidentally left open the glass door to the comfortable, temperature-controlled room in which the young nine-foot regal python mostly lived.

The evening began with Lupe and the young forgetful listening to the parental instructions given by the forgetful parents. Then, in a flurry of kisses and hugs, the parents waved good-bye. From the front door, Lupe and Little Forgetful waved back, then closed the front door, and wandered through the house, heading for the pool. Along the way, the forgetful kid picked up a bowl of fresh peaches from the kitchen, offered Lupe one. Lupe said no thanks right now but later I'd love one. The kid mumbled something about maybe not being any left later, which Lupe took as a sort of boast, for there must have been twenty peaches in that bowl.

The kid, to Lupe's mild surprise, carried the bowl along toward the garden. Lupe, who, along with me and five others, spends her summer days working as a lifeguard and swimming instructor at our local pool, then took the forgetful kid swimming in the family's purple pool.

Sleepy as she was, Lupe noticed that the kid was definitely acting strange. Whatever he did, wherever he went, he kept that bowl of peaches nearby. Lupe assumed the kid had somehow become afraid of the water. Tired as she was, she tried real hard to put him at ease during their swim, but Little Forgetful kept avoiding her eyes, looking past her all the time. From an adult that sort of behavior is infuriating, from a kid Lupe found it a tad creepy.

From the pool they went to the pool house to dry themselves and change, then back to the kitchen to cook up some pasta for supper.

The kid never took a step without that bowl of peaches. Lupe did wonder how the kid had ever latched on to such a strange comfort. I mean, we all know about favorite teddy bears, or thumb-sucking, or a favorite blanket or pillow, but a bowl of peaches? Lupe marveled at that one.

After supper it was checkers and sixty other board games, and ten or so books read aloud, with the kid holding that bowl of peaches and always looking around, so tense. Tired as she was, and slow to respond, Lupe felt it was the strangest evening she ever had spent. Finally, it was bedtime. The forgetful kid went willingly, taking the peaches along. Carefully, he removed his lamp from the bedside table and put it on the floor.

"The peaches need room," he told Lupe with a serious face. Lupe just shrugged. Then the kid lay down, facing the bowl of peaches.

Lupe said good night, then went down to putter in the kitchen. She was so tired she did not dare to sit down, for fear she'd fall asleep before the kid did. After she had washed and tidied the already clean and tidy kitchen, and straightened every volume on the cookbook shelf, Lupe went back upstairs to check on Little Forgetful.

He was asleep, his face just three inches from the bowl of peaches. Lupe, wondering if maybe the kid was addicted to the sweet smell of ripe peaches, picked up the bowl, put the lamp back on the table, and, helping herself to a peach, headed back downstairs. In the TV room, she put the peaches on the coffee table, put herself on the couch, sitting bolt upright, eating, with a napkin in her hand, an absolutely delicious peach. Lupe thought she could fight off the tiredness that enveloped her, but sleep won out over even the taste of a summer-ripe peach.

That unfinished peach in her right hand, Lupe

slumped, then sank, then stretched out full length on the TV room sofa. Lupe slept, and dreamed of whispers, of the sighs of pine trees in the wind; the words of poems and songs whispered all around her, soft sounds, of a hand smoothing a silk dress, and all the while sweet sleep.

After some time, the dreams changed to ones of sports, of tennis, and racquetball, of rowing, of hauling lines on a huge sailboat. In these dreams Lupe worked hard, swam, climbed, hoisted huge net bags of soccer balls, worked so hard that finally she found herself in that state of being almost awake.

It was then that Lupe saw, through eyes half open, the room, the coffee table, the couch, herself on the couch, and Lupe saw that she was not alone.

On the coffee table, the bowl of peaches was empty. On the sofa, the body of a glistening regal python was coiled ever so gently around Lupe, with the head of the young and somewhat greedy snake nudging gently but persistently against Lupe's hand, the sticky right hand that held that last, not-quite-eaten peach.

Even in her sleepy state, Lupe perceived that the python wanted the peach. Lupe, never one to scream or faint, opened her hand and gave it to him.

Poppy

On Friday, Poppy was done with school forever. On Monday morning pretty darned early, Poppy's mother handed Poppy the want ads and pushed her out the door, saying, "Find a school or find a job. Today."

That's how Poppy came to be the baby-sitter for the Banner children, all four of them. Their mama, Mrs. Banner, had up and died, leaving Mr. Banner with the four little ones, ages two, three, four, and five. Poppy thought that of all the possible jobs she might have to get, baby-sitting certainly would be the easiest. For sure, she could do the job sitting down. After all, the Banners, tightfisted as old Mr. Banner was, did have a large television set.

And that's the way it was. Poppy got the job. Mr. Banner went out the front door. Poppy turned on the television set and sat herself down to watch. The four Banner children, who had grown pretty wild during their mother's illness, continued as they had been doing.

That whole first day, and the second, and the third, Poppy took her eyes off the television screen only when she made herself something to eat. Because there was not a single clean knife in the kitchen, Poppy used a spoon to scoop peanut butter out of the jar onto a piece of bread. Because there was not a single clean mug or glass, Poppy drank from her hands, which she cupped under the kitchen faucet, noticing as she did so that the kitchen sink, like all the others in the house, smelled of urine.

Stepping carefully around the lumps of food, worms of toothpaste, remains of dirty diapers, and unidentifiable splotches on the kitchen floor, Poppy wiped her wet hands on the legs of her jeans. She wished Mr. Banner would buy some soda for her to drink, but of course he wouldn't. Mr. Banner was known to be pretty tightfisted.

And that is how Mr. Banner came to court Poppy. When he got home at night, he could see that Poppy had done nothing all day but sit. Mr. Banner wanted Poppy to cook and clean, to wash and iron, but he knew Poppy wouldn't so long as she was paid only to baby-sit. Mr. Banner could not bear to part with enough money to pay someone to do all the work that needed to be done in that house. As it was, it pained Mr. Banner terribly to pay Poppy, or anyone else, to baby-sit.

Poppy was young. Mr. Banner was sure he could train her to be a good wife. As a good wife, Poppy would work for free.

After Poppy had been baby-sitting for a few days, Mr. Banner set out to charm Poppy just as he had charmed the young girl who had become Mrs. Banner all those years ago.

And, as long as it did not cost any money, Mr. Banner could be very charming. Mr. Banner praised Poppy until she blushed. Mr. Banner said that Poppy deserved a wedding ring of gold, a gold ring heavy with diamonds, so heavy it would take both her hands to lift the hand that wore it. His smile was bright when he said it, his eyes full of the sadness of love. Poppy laughed, sighed to picture herself so laden with diamonds that she could not raise a hand to work.

Mr. Banner knew exactly the look of the ring he was describing. It was the ring Mrs. Banner had worn, still wore. It was the ring Mrs. Banner was given by her grandmother when she married Mr. Banner, who had with immense charm convinced the family that he was good, noble in fact, but too poor in worldly goods to provide a ring for his bride.

Poor Mrs. Banner suffered for years in her marriage to the tightwad who so charmed his babysitter. Oh yes. Mrs. Banner had been worn to death by the sleazy skinflint who described her wedding ring to a breathless Poppy.

And that ring? It could be found easily enough, in a grave, on the third finger of the left hand of the Mrs. Banner who lay wrapped in her shroud. With her last breath she had clasped her hands, and had not opened them when Mr. Banner tried to get the ring from her finger. After that moment, it had been impossible for him to take the ring. There were people who could see, and others who knew that Mrs. Banner insisted she be buried with the ring. After all, it was her very own. For Mr. Banner at the time, it had been only a small problem. After all, he knew where to find the ring when the time came to take it.

Now. Now was the time. First, Mr. Banner charmed Poppy into accepting his offer of marriage. After that it was an easy matter to convince her that only that particular ring of gold, heavy with diamonds, would do as a wedding ring for Poppy.

Together they would fetch the ring. Poppy agreed.

Together they drove out of town, up the hill to the old cemetery.

Together they carried their shovels along the path, around one tombstone after another, to the place where Mrs. Banner lay, no tombstone above her head. Together they dug away at the soil above the body. Six feet down, they touched the body; no coffin for Mrs. Banner. Together they brushed away at the dirt, unwrapped the shroud.

Mrs. Banner lay, hands clasped, the gold of the ring glowing softly even there deep in the ground. The diamonds sparkled, even there deep in the ground.

Together Poppy and Mr. Banner tried, tried with all the force they could muster, to pry open those fingers, to slip the ring over the knuckle of that dead hand.

The hands held fast. The ring remained on that finger. Together they sweated in the chill night air, gritting their teeth, pulling at those fingers with all their might. At last Mr. Banner let go of the hand, reached into his pocket for a knife.

"No," said Poppy. "That won't do. Use the edge of the shovel."

Together, they used the shovel to chop the finger from the hand. At last, the ring was free.

Breathless, Poppy slipped it onto her finger. How beautiful it was. Even down there, deep in the earth, crouched over that corpse, you could see how spectacular a ring it was.

"Lovely, isn't it?" asked the first Mrs. Banner, as she reached up to clasp both of them, together, to her breast.

They struggled, oh how Mr. Banner and Poppy struggled, but the first Mrs. Banner was stronger than both of them.

They sobbed. They pleaded. Poppy pulled at the ring, trying to wrench it from her finger. She tried to give it back, but the ring did not budge. Mrs. Banner held them fast. The earth fell in upon them, as she dragged them down, down, down, together, with her forever.

Life as a 900 Number

Bloke was your basic problem child. At twelve years of age he was sweaty, crafty, an outrageous liar, and he very much needed to be baby-sat. Sure, his parents pretended they got some older guy to come over to hang out with Bloke for an evening "so the kid won't be lonely," but the truth was they had to pay a fortune to get anybody, and they sure could not leave Bloke alone in the house, ever!

The trouble Bloke got into, the trouble he caused, was limitless. For one thing, that cunning Bloke, the minute there was a sitter in the house; well, Bloke got right on the wire, making fast and furious use of 900 numbers on his parents' telephone. When the bills for those calls came in, Bloke's mother and father yelled to blue blazes about those rotten sitters. And there stood Bloke looking like a little kid who had never even heard of 900 numbers and had no idea at all what his parents were talking about. *Sure* his parents assumed the calls had been made by the sitter. After all, 900 calls only happened when there was a sitter in the house. Bloke's parents paid for those 900 calls, cursing all the while, and punished the one they assumed was guilty, the sitter, by never calling him or her again.

Last night Bloke's parents went to the opera, which was followed by a late supper. The sitter last night was a new guy, a sturdy youth, a six-foot-four-inch vegetarian. He, his backpack of home-work, and his immense appetite, arrived at 6:30, in time to have dinner with Bloke. Bloke, whose seven basic foods included Twinkies and marsh-mallows in all possible combinations, watched in awed revulsion as the sitter chopped raw vegetables on the kitchen block.

Bloke's parents departed for the opera, sighing at the contrast between their son and the young giant, while at the same time hoping the two might hit it off, might in fact become friends. There was a wishful parental hope. Perhaps the next five or six years could bring that sort of person out of their Bloke?

As soon as their car left the drive, Bloke ceased chatting up the sitter with a series of questions that had revealed that the sturdy youth played bare-knuckle Native American lacrosse, had grown up playing it, and yes he played college lacrosse as well.

Bloke ducked out of the kitchen, sauntered upstairs to make the first of his planned series of 900 calls. He returned to the kitchen just seven minutes later, when the sitter called him for dinner. Bloke tasted the stir-fry, praised the stir-fry, and abandoned the stir-fry to make another call.

In this way, the evening passed. The sitter engaged in several assaults on the contents of the refrigerator, on the bowl of fruit on the dining-room table, and upon the loaf of bread on the kitchen counter. Bloke conversed with the sitter, offered access to the stereo, and played a few hands of poker with the sitter. Also, Bloke excused himself every now and again to go upstairs. The sitter assumed Bloke was weak in the bladder. Bloke did a fine job of giving that impression, all the while making his 900 calls.

At last Bloke bade the sitter good night, saying he was tired. The sitter, obviously relieved to be free of Bloke's company, sat down to the dining-room table with his textbooks.

Upstairs, Bloke carried his parents' telephone into his room. There he dialed the last 900 number on his list, the number that promised to satisfy any desire, any compulsion. From under the covers of his bed, Bloke dialed, listened while voices told him of power, words of satisfaction, words that held him in their grip, words that compelled him to listen on and on and on. Bloke's eyes grew wide, wide with fear that became terror; and still the words flowed unceasingly out of the receiver into his ear, into his brain and body. Bloke's veins burst into flame, his muscles contorted in agony. Bloke could not release the receiver. His cry for help strangled before it reached his lips.

When the sitter, at about midnight, looked in on Bloke, he saw only a little kid, peacefully in bed, a still form under a thin blanket. The sitter saw no telephone, no lights that needed to be turned out. The sitter closed the door and returned to his studies.

When they arrived at his bedside intending to kiss their sleeping son good night, Bloke's parents found the phone clutched in Bloke's cold hand, the connection unbroken, the voices of the 900 number still talking, at something more than nine dollars a minute.

Sitting in Egypt

/ was ten years old in 1981, old enough to hang around my big cousin Pete and his friend, listening to their stories of the Peace Corps, getting completely caught up in their obsession with the pyramids. They loved hiking; they loved the Arabic language and the foods and music of the Middle East, and they loved talking by the hour. Pete had come to our house for a visit, and his buddy Morgan dropped by one day in the second week of Pete's stay. My father, who was working for our government, assigned to a mission in Egypt, was gone a lot, so Pete and Morgan settled in as sort of baby-sitters for me, since the servants pretty much let me do anything I wanted, and my father felt I needed more supervision than that.

Dad was gone, back home for an assignment that would last a month or more. I had said no thanks to the trip. I was happier in Cairo with Pete and Morgan. I went with them climbing the pyramids, inside, outside, and around. They talked and talked, and I listened, all ears, while they indulged in their fantasy. They would spend a night inside a pyramid.

They chose a day, and made their plans, forgetting completely that I listened and that I intended to be with them. Out of respect for the tombs and for the ancients who had built them, they would carry neither food nor drink along with them, and would take away no memento, not so much as a chip of stone or clay. They had studied the routines of the guards, so they knew just how and when they could manage to elude them. They were going to do it, to spend a night in a pyramid.

On the chosen day, I was there, right beside my cousin Pete. He tried to send me home, but I pleaded, and they gave in. They knew I could climb and not ever complain.

We took the last tour of the day, lingering, lingering, until we had been left far behind. Cautiously, we made it to the spot Pete and Morgan had chosen. We concealed ourselves as best we could, and waited. The guards' normal routine was

37

to check the passages and chambers before closing and locking all entrances and exits for the night. We planned that, after the guards had left, we would separate, each to be alone to sit and think and listen, as one does in the wilderness. We would *attend* the whole night long.

For half an hour or more, we crouched in the dark as we listened to the footsteps of the guards, up one corridor, down another. At last a single guard approached. I held my breath. He walked past me, past Morgan, past my cousin Pete. Just a few minutes more, and he would be gone. As I silently counted his footsteps, the guard reached out his hand, and struck a match on the wall not three inches from Pete's face. Both the guard and Pete flinched, drawing in breath loudly. The guard dropped the match, and the cigarette he had been preparing to light.

At that, Morgan and Pete put into operation the second part of their plan. They offered the guard a bribe. At first he refused, then said that we could stay the night for one hundred American dollars. To the three of us, the sum was immense. Sadly, we followed the guard out of the pyramid. He, his rounds still not complete, returned to the inside, after he had locked us out.

Without a word, we walked away from the site. Night had fallen. The area around the pyramids was deserted. There was not a single taxi, not a bus, not a car, not anyone on foot. It was strange, but in our defeated mood, we did not talk, but instead began to walk.

We walked and walked and walked, and at a certain point Morgan and Pete began to recite in Arabic. I listened. Odd how they started together, as if they had agreed upon it, to recite some lines by al-Jahiz, written in about 800. "A man who is noble does not pretend to be noble, any more than an eloquent man feigns eloquence . . . Cruelty is the worst of sins, and humility is better than clemency, which is the best of good deeds."

When they repeated it, I joined them, and then we fell silent. It was not a night for singing as you walked, not when the streets were deserted.

On and on we walked, never seeing a soul. It was far from Giza to home, far. We were blistered and tired when we got there. The servants were surprised, not that they had known of our plan. No. They were not themselves, and so whatever we did amazed them in their grief. While we had been at Giza, the president of Egypt, Anwar el-

Sadat, had been assassinated. All of Egypt was closed down, in mourning, and in fear of violence. The pyramids, once closed and locked that night, did not open again for two weeks.

This is a true story.

Sit!

After six months in Rome, Isabella had achieved fairly decent conversational Italian, and an invitation to tea. The invitation was important, for Isabella had come to Rome dreaming that she would meet an aristocrat, and she had.

Isabella was an American girl, so lovely to look at that it stopped your breath the first time you saw her. Along with her beauty, she was gentle. Because of the joy people took in her presence, very little had ever been asked of Isabella.

There, in Rome, shortly after she arrived for what her not-very-demanding college called "the junior year abroad," Isabella met a charming, handsome, very aristocratic Italian gentleman. That gentleman, like everyone else, was enchanted with Isabella, so enchanted that he did a very serious thing. He invited Isabella to tea, to meet his mama and his grandmama in their family apartment in

Rome. In old-fashioned families in Italy, such an invitation announces that the young man wishes to marry the young lady. And, in old-fashioned families in Italy, marriage is a very serious matter.

On the appointed afternoon, Isabella, who was never nervous about any social engagement, went calmly, cheerfully, to meet Mama and Grandmama. She liked the apartment, which seemed ancient and vast, with ceilings nearly as high as a cathedral, and doors to match. Tea was served in a room in which there stood no fewer than four sofas, each one covered in softly faded silk, each one crowded with squashy pillows. There were, as well, innumerable lamps, tables, and chairs. Grandmama sat on one chair, Mama in another. Mama poured, while maids wove through the crowd bearing plates, cups, saucers. And there was a crowd. There were cousins and aunts and uncles, standing, sitting, walking, talking. The tea drinkers were divided into two camps. There were those who drank it strong, after the English fashion. They had spared no effort to determine exactly which blend of tea best suited the water from their aqueduct. Most of the English camp drank their tea with milk, some with sugar as well. In the second camp were those who drank tea _bionde,_ blond, in the Roman fashion. The blond tea was more yellow than brown, drunk usually with lemon and sugar. Isabella sat on one of the sofas, where she got on quite well with the cousins seated on either side of her. Isabella's young man, everyone could see how completely in love with her he was, hovered.

Isabella, after one cup of tea, did something no well-brought up European young lady would ever do. She asked the girl cousin sitting next to her if she could use the bathroom. The cousin, as well-brought up as any young lady in all of Europe, was mildly surprised at the request. She shrugged, for everyone knew Americans were a bit peculiar. Because Isabella had used the word "bathroom," the cousin assumed that Isabella needed to wash her hands or reassure herself of the perfection of her looks in the mirror. Courteously, she escorted Isabella out of the salon and down a corridor to a bathroom.

Once inside, Isabella immediately saw her mistake. The room held a sink and a gigantic ancient bathtub. Isabella decided that she could not seek out the cousin to admit her mistake. Neither could she wander up and down the corridor looking for the toilet, so Isabella decided that it was after all a small matter. She would use the sink.

Outside the bathroom door, the cousin hesitated. Should she wait for Isabella, or return to the others?

The girl cousin had taken a few steps up the hall when she heard the crash.

In the bathroom, the sink had torn away from the wall, and fallen, along with Isabella, to the floor. Isabella, who had hit her head on the bathtub, lay beside the sink, unconscious.

When Isabella awoke, it was in bed in a room in a hospital in Rome. Already, the room was full of flowers, sent by the adoring young man of aristocratic family.

There were a few whispers on the fringes of the family, those who asked how it was that the sink, which had stood there for such a very long time, should choose to fall when Isabella came to visit. Nevertheless, after she had recovered from her slight concussion, Isabella was once again invited back to the apartment for tea. On this second visit there were fewer cousins, but Grandmama had brought along her lap dogs. There were two of them, both silvery blond, two little mops on the floor, though they preferred to nap on one or another of the sofas.

During tea, Isabella behaved flawlessly. She drank tea. She ate small *biscotti*. When others spoke to her in Italian, she listened and smiled and agreed in all the right places. All in all, her young man had every reason to be enchanted. With joy he noticed that Mama and Grandmama seemed pleased with Isabella.

After a time, the young man and one of the girl cousins took Isabella to look at some of the family paintings. When they returned, Isabella sat down on one of the satin sofas. Anyone would have agreed that Isabella sat down gently enough, but still, everyone in the room heard a bleat. Isabella jumped up. Everyone looked. Isabella lifted a squashy satin pillow. There lay one of Grandmama's little dogs. With the pillow out of the way, everyone could see that the little dog was dead.

This, too, is a true story.

Toads and Slime

Gertruda was a five-year-old girl standing, tired, hot, and cranky, in a crowded supermarket, waiting for her mother. As she waited, Gertruda twisted a strand of her long dark hair.

"Little girl!" an adult voice commanded. "Stop twisting your hair!"

Crabby Gertruda did not stop twisting her hair, but did close her eyes and stick out her tongue in the general direction of the adult voice.

In a crash of thunder, Gertruda heard herself cursed: "From your mouth, you rude little girl, will come forth toads, newts, and other creatures, every time you open your lips to speak. And from your hair, every time you touch it with your hands, will come snakes, bats, and other flying creatures. And you will be called Toads and Slime. This curse will remain until someone can love you in spite of your loathsome issue!!!"

Afterward, Toads and Slime grew to be a woman, silent and solitary. Even though she never spoke, and never put her hands to her hair, there was about her something of Toads and Slime, more than just the name, which even her mother was forced to speak, though she tried with all her might never to say it.

We knew nothing of her story until the time of our own troubles. It began with the love and optimism of my mother and father. When I was a cheerful two-year-old, they asked me what I wanted for my birthday. I replied that I wanted brothers and sisters, lots and lots and lots of them. I showed all my fingers as I spoke. My parents, who were themselves fond of brothers and sisters, set out to make for us a large family, adopting foundlings and orphans until we were twelve in all. (Two times the orphans were twins.) What my parents had not thought about — none of us had — was death. When I was twelve, they both died, struck by lightning while trying to keep the roof on the barn in a bad storm.

The committee that came out to our house said

our parents were worthless hippies, and we a bunch of ragamuffins. "If we had the proper sort of orphanages these days," thundered one of the committee, "then we could send the lot of you there to see what could be made of you!" Someone else whispered, and believe me I listened, and heard them say the best would be to sell off all of our land but the swamp, which they called dismal, and hire someone so awful they could get her cheap, and then we would all be out of sight and out of mind, and our taxes *would be paid in advance*. The committee members shook hands on us, and the land was sold and a sitter engaged, and each of us children got a stamp on the back of our right hand. It was a circle of purple ink, with the words "Government Inspected: Certified Orphans" written inside.

The next morning, a truck pulled up to our gate. A woman, dressed all in black, stood up. She threw a tattered bag off the back of the truck, which barely paused to let her climb down. We watched her carry her bag down the lane to our house. She looked grim.

The first few days Toads and Slime did not speak, not a word. She cooked and cleaned, changed diapers, and did laundry. And I will say for all of us kids, we had done a fair job before she got there, and continued to work after she arrived, but many hands make light work, so it was good to have the help. She, by the terms of her contract, was supposed to school us, so that the fine people of the county should not have to deal with the likes of us sharing a schoolroom or playground with their children.

Toads and Slime wrote to us, using paper, a blackboard; and wonder of wonders, she could sign. We could too, all of us, because one of the foundlings had been made deaf by a sickness, so our parents had learned, and taught us all. Sign she could, but Toads and Slime was no fun. No; not a smile, not a joke, not a pun, and we were not used to this grim life, not at all.

It might have gone on that way forever, but one day I made our spaghetti sauce a bit . . . hmmm, what shall I say? I had been sort of daydreaming and chopping garlic and got carried away. When I saw what I had chopped, I shrugged and dumped it into the pan. I mean, whoever heard of too much garlic?

After dinner Toads and Slime got the hiccups. She tried to run out of the room, but with twelve kids underfoot she could not. She tried to cover her mouth, but the hiccups were too much for her. We watched as out of her mouth came hopping

toads, slugs and snails, and newts, and oh my good-
ness every creature the swamp loves. We were de-
lighted! The baby laughed for the first time since
our parents' funeral. All of us laughed until we
cried, and we hugged Toads and Slime, who put
her hands to her face, touching her hair, so that
bats flew up, and snakes came out, and animals and
children filled the room, until everyone went outside, where the animals were much happier.

Now you may think it cruel, but cranes and her-
ons and all the birds of the swamp quickly learned
to come around whenever Toads and Slime took
a walk in the marshes. They waited for her to
sneeze, or speak, or sing, or anything, because dinner was right there.

And we all loved the lumpy bumpy toads, always
had, always will. And we loved our Toads and
Slime, though we made sure the committee members never knew.

Years passed, and we grew up, and we wondered
wasn't it time the curse was lifted. And so we filled
out all the appropriate paperwork, and believe me
it is tons and tons of it, all in triplicate. We re-
quested that the curse be lifted from Toads and
Slime because we loved her.

It took months, but the answer was no. We ap-
pealed, three times, and finally got a hearing. There

was testimony, and the answer came back that the curse could not be lifted because we did not love Toads and Slime *in spite* of the loathsome things that issued from her mouth and hair, but *because* of them, and so she must remain cursed. It was tough because, strictly speaking, they were correct. In time, however, we received a note from the judge saying that there would be a modification of the curse. We had, in fact, noticed the change already.

From almost that first case of hiccups, there had been butterflies and moths among the creatures that issued from the mouth and hair of Toads and Slime. Now, day by day, there were more and more, until these splendid, fragile, colorful creatures outnumbered the toads and frogs and snakes. The ever-hungry birds were disappointed, but it was easier on our Toads and Slime. We now can say, sometimes, and we never know which words will come out, but we can call her Gertruda. She says that the creatures issuing forth are not so bad. They remind her not to take herself too seriously.

Double Pay

*I*t was a bad time. My parents had died in the spring, leaving debts and me, one skinny thirteen-year-old. Doing her duty, Aunt Rose took me in. We were a gloomy and silent pair. To me, it seemed Aunt Rose begrudged every mouthful of food I took; and oh, the way she watched me. I'd take clean sheets from the closet, turn, and there she'd be, standing at the kitchen door.

"Clean sheets?"

When she said it, I felt she was criticizing. I wanted to defend myself, but I wasn't sure from the sound of her voice if she thought I changed them too often or too seldom. Not knowing what to say, I'd avoid her eyes, grunt, and go about my business. The place was tiny, so it wasn't easy to keep out of her way.

Aunt Rose worked hard for her living. That was

what people said, "Rose works hard for her living."

For me, that was just one more thing to feel bad about. Sure, I tried to help. I worked at whatever jobs I could, and gave Aunt Rose every penny I earned.

The jobs, which were mostly baby-sitting, also served to keep me out of the house. Aunt Rose lived in an old subdivision of double houses called "duplexes" that bordered on a newer subdivision of single houses. The new houses were full of babies and little kids; for me, the subdivision was full of baby-sitting jobs. Of course, Aunt Rose made a rule that I could only sit for people if she had the name, address, and telephone number, and if she knew the people or knew the person who had recommended me. If somebody called with a recommendation, Aunt Rose got right on the phone to check, every single time. In spite of what I felt was her intrusive overprotection, in the six months I had lived with her, I had built up quite a business.

Over Saturday morning coffee in her kitchen, friends of Aunt Rose would gather to whisper that I was sullen. Hearing them, I'd scowl past, off to a baby-sitting job.

Then, one Thursday night while Aunt Rose was

out getting her hair done, a stranger telephoned, and I broke my aunt's rule. A man called, a man I did not know, a man with a whisper so creepy it made my hair crawl, a man who said he needed a sitter in half an hour; and I said yes.

When the man arrived, less than half an hour later, the sallow, scruffy look of him was not more reassuring than his voice. Quickly, before my aunt could return to prevent me, I went out and shut the door behind me. On the kitchen table I had left her a note: "Gone baby-sitting." I gave no name, no address, no telephone number. I never even asked.

In silence, the man drove me to a house in the newer subdivision. When I saw the place, I could only think how much the neighbors must detest these people. All around, as far as you could see, the lawns were tidy, green all winter long. On every street, neighbor vied against neighbor to have the finest shrubs and trees. Some opted for flowers, others for a more formal look, but one and all criticized anyone who dared to "let the place go."

"This way," the man whispered, leading me up a sidewalk that divided two plots of clay studded with gray weeds. Alongside the foundations of the house, dry sticks remained of whatever shrubs had once been planted. There was no trace of the sap-

ling the developer had put in front of every house
in that subdivision. Inside was freezing cold, and
smelled of wet cement. The living room held one
single piece of furniture, a hard yellow couch. The
only light came from a ceiling fixture. From the
kitchen, a woman came, buttoning her coat, eyes
down as if the act required all of her concentration.
Without a word, the man led me past her, down
the hall into a bedroom, which held a crib. There,
asleep, was a scrawny baby of about six months.

"We will be back in two hours," the man whispered. "It's a meeting." The woman, who had not
said a word, opened the front door.

"Should I feed the baby?" I asked, knowing full
well that I should be asking for a telephone number
where I could reach them.

"Oh, he never wakes in the night." With that
last whisper, the man closed the door behind them.

Hunching into my jacket, I nevertheless went
into the kitchen to check the refrigerator for any
possible bottle of baby formula or milk they might
have left for the baby, and yes there was one lone
bottle in that nearly empty box.

Feeling that two hours was going to seem like a
very long time, I sat down on the couch to begin
my homework. In spite of the cold and the rotten
light, it went pretty well. I was nearly finished

when the baby started to cry. I left him for a minute or so, waiting to see if he would fall back to
sleep. Some of them did that, cry out, then settle
down so long as you left them alone. It could be
hell to pick up one of those babies too soon. But,
with this baby, the cries got louder and more in-
tense. I walked down the hall to his room.

Poor little guy. He was the ugliest baby I'd ever
seen, skinny, with a long thin neck and bony head,
no hair, and big staring eyes. I talked to him, told
him I'd check his diaper first. He reeked of urine,
but the diaper was dry. I picked him up, talked
nice to him, rubbed his back, swayed and rocked
with him, walked with him. His cries mounted as
if he were afraid. I stayed with it, walking, talking,
and slowly he grew quiet, but remained stiff in my
arms. Through that chilly house we walked, me
looking for a clock. It had to be time for them to
come home.

The baby gradually began to relax and I to hope
he'd fall asleep, but then he stiffened again and began to shriek. I'd never heard a baby cry like that,
never. It made me want to scream. Talking softly,
swaying, I carried him into the kitchen, warmed
the bottle, but the baby refused to drink it. I tried
burping him, tried bicycling his legs, but nothing
worked. He cried so long and so hard that I felt

anger growing inside me. I wanted to — well, I did not listen to what I wanted to do — but just put back the bottle and started to walk and sway, sway and talk, telling the kid songs, and prayers we'd learned in French class; told that baby everything I could think of. The cries subsided, but still the kid was stiff, as if he was scared.

It had to have been hours later when he finally went to sleep, me nearly asleep myself as I rubbed his back while he lay in his crib. After he got quiet, I went back to the living room to that ugly hard couch to see if I could finish my homework. Even without a clock, I knew I was in for big trouble with Aunt Rose for being out so late. In spite of the homework, the cold, and knowing I was going to catch it from Aunt Rose, I fell asleep.

When I opened my eyes, the man's face was inches from mine. He was kneeling there, staring at me. The woman, standing behind him, was crying, her eyes holding mine with tears streaming down her cheeks. Terrified, I sat up, scrabbled for my books, desperate to be out of there, muttering that I was sorry I'd fallen asleep.

"Oh, that's all right," the man whispered, adding that they had not planned to be so late. He paid me double what I usually charged, whispering his thanks and that they'd like to call me again. I was saying yes but thinking no and opening the door before he could do it for me. The outside air tasted so good, but from my jacket came the smell of the house, cold wet cement and cold, wet ashes. During the ride home, I pressed myself into the car door, not sure I'd ever get there. But then I saw the porch light, and dashed out of the car as soon as it stopped.

Inside, I left half the money for Aunt Rose, thinking that of this job at least one good thing had come, some money of my own. As quietly as I could, I went to bed. Aunt Rose never waited up. From the beginning she'd said she couldn't, not if she had to be at work at seven in the morning.

The next morning at breakfast Aunt Rose said, "I expected more from you."

"You mean money?" I gasped, thinking that somehow she knew what I'd been paid.

"No. Responsibility."

I felt both good and bad, relieved that she'd said so little, but bad that I felt guilty about the money.

After school I walked home a different way so I could pass that house, the one where I'd been the night before. I wanted to see, from the safety of the opposite side of the street, if it looked as awful in the daylight as it had at night.

At first, I couldn't find it. I walked the block

twice, looking. Wondering if I had somehow got the wrong street, I approached a lady sitting on her front porch watching a toddler push a small carriage up and down the front walk. She smiled; I asked her if there was a house on that street, probably rented, where the people didn't take care of the yard.

"It *was* there." She pointed to a grassy vacant lot diagonally across the street.

I must have looked really dumb.

"It burned down three years ago. There is some sort of court case to settle before anyone can build there again."

She looked down at her toddler, then at me. "It was awful. Two babies died in the fire. It went so fast."

"Two babies?" I asked.

"One less than a year, the other nearly three." She turned her face from me, watched her toddler intently. I started to walk away, but she continued. "I wish they'd make a park there, not a house. Who'd want to live there?"

I turned back. The lady's voice was cracking.

"I heard the babies cry." She raised her hands, then dropped them into her lap. "If only they had asked someone for help."

"I don't understand."

"No. Of course. You see, they kept to themselves, never took care of the garden. No one knew, but they must have been struggling. He worked days; she worked nights. He'd drive every night at midnight to pick her up from work. He'd leave those babies asleep alone in the house. The night of the fire, he'd picked up his wife from the cannery, and on the ride home they got hit from behind by a truck. The trucker said they didn't have rear lights. He said he never saw them."

The toddler abandoned the carriage, ran up, and started pulling at her mother's skirt. The woman opened her arms, took the kid onto her lap.

"In the house, the fire started, went so fast. The babies died in the fire, the parents in the wreck of the car."

At this point the toddler started to whine. The woman took the kid's hands, made patty-cake, whispered, tickled the kid's face with her eyelashes while she whispered "butterfly kiss." The kid laughed, glad her mother had stopped talking to a stranger.

I said thanks and 'bye. When she was sure I was leaving, the toddler looked at me.

The lady said, "I still hear those babies cry, sometimes, at night."

I went home, not liking the feel of that baby-sitting money, the half I had held back from Aunt Rose, in my pocket. When my aunt got home, I offered it to her, saying the people had been so late they gave me a bonus, which I'd forgotten to give to her.

Aunt Rose didn't even look up from the evening paper. "Keep it. A kid your age needs some pocket money."

Well, I didn't want it. I'd never think of anything that money could give me. All the next day I fiddled and figured, wondering if I should just slip it into Aunt Rose's purse. But that would never work. She knew exactly how much she had, and besides, if she saw me, she might think I was snooping or stealing. After a whole day of back and forth with one idea and another, I bought Aunt Rose some flowers. My father always said flowers in a vase were the one luxury my mother desired. The bouquet was nice, really pretty, but still there was some money left. I went through agonies of indecision all over again before I bought Aunt Rose a used paperback joke book. Then I got such cold feet on the way home that I nearly chucked both gifts into a garbage can.

As it turned out, Aunt Rose was glad. She fussed with the flowers, climbing up to reach into the back of the highest cupboard in the kitchen for a vase. She thanked me, reached out as if she might touch me. I probably flinched, as I had always done with her, and Aunt Rose held back.

After dinner, she started to read aloud from the joke book. Some of them were pretty corny, but we laughed anyway.

"Gotta save a few for tomorrow." Aunt Rose sighed, taking off her glasses and wiping her eyes. "Ya know; some of these are wheezers my uncle told me when I was your age."

I started to clear the table.

"He's the uncle . . . did your father ever tell you about him? He used to take out his false teeth, top and bottom, the whole set, and clack them at us kids. We'd fall on the ground laughing, but scared, too." Before I went to bed that night, I gave my Aunt Rose a hug, a small sort of half-an-arm's-length hug. It wasn't so bad, and it made her smile.

Between the two of us, things got better after that. When her friends came for coffee, I made sure to scowl and leave, 'cause I hated it so much when they said, loud enough for me to hear, how nice it was that I had gotten nicer. I did not blame Aunt Rose for them. I knew she didn't gossip about me; that was one of the good things about how quiet she was.

Still, I never told her about that night, though I

brooded about it often enough, and even reached a few conclusions.

Then, a year later to the day, when I heard that creepy whisper on the telephone, I knew my conclusions were right.

"Thank you. My wife and I both thank you. Can you help us just once more? Can you come tonight to comfort our three-year-old? It won't be for long, not so long as last time. The baby suffered terribly for such a long time. But our daughter lasted only a little while."

Cat-Bit

sk not my name, age, sex, nor previous condition. Nothing is as it was. Oh yes. I had power. I believed I did, believed, too, that I knew about cats. I believed I possessed them; I believed I "owned" them.

I went down to the ocean, to that many-windowed house just past the dunes, to be a caretaker, a "sitter" for the house and the cats. It was a simple task, full of the pleasure of the ocean, the deserted beaches, the sky, the wind, the waving grasses. Those pleasures, at least, remain.

On that certain morning, I awoke slowly, stretching, feeling the cool sheets against my skin. The window beside the bed was open to the breezes from the sea, and to the light from the dawn sky. During the night, the door to my room must have silently swung shut. Certainly it had not made enough noise to awaken me, light sleeper that I was. The cat I called my own was standing there, next to that closed door. Oh yes. I should have paid attention to where she was looking, but I did not.

Instead, I swung my feet to the floor. As I did, I heard from beneath the bed a terrifying growl, the sound of a cat beside itself with anger.

Still I did nothing to save myself, but continued as I had been doing, getting out of bed to stand there in the room. As I stood up, feeling for my slippers with my feet, I looked around the room. I saw that on the windowsill there sat yet another cat, a stranger to me.

With the first bite into the soft flesh of my foot, I gained a clear perception of the situation. The cat who lived in that seaside house had never liked me, a fact I had accepted with no rancor. The cat who lived in that house was the one that shot out from beneath the bed to bite into my heel not once, not twice, but three times. By the third bite, I had cried out quite loudly in pain, and I had managed to open the door from the room.

My cry had also caused the cat on the windowsill to leap out, away from my voice. To the resident cat, I was the dangerous intruder who had trapped it in a room under a bed with enemies at the closed door and at the open window, while placing my own two feet in the middle of the room. Well, by the third bite, my cries and my opening of the door made it possible for that cat to leap up and out the window.

By that third bite, I was all but blind with pain. Four small puncture wounds glistened with my ruby blood. Two more were invisible.

Until the owner of the seaside house returned, I soaked and nursed the foot, and avoided the cat as best I could. Upon returning to my own home, I looked long and hard at my swollen and painful heel. There was no denying I needed the help of a doctor. She gave me antibiotics and sympathy, expressing concern that I had not sought help immediately, for cats, she told me, can give you a nasty infection. She, of course, had no way of knowing.

One sort of infection healed, but the other result of those bites is for all time.

The changes have been going on for weeks. I can feel that it is near the end, so I have made my way back to the seaside, to the home of my master. That cat is much kinder to me now, kinder, the others tell me, than many masters are to their apprentices.

The former friend, the human who owns this house, noticed me yesterday. She told her sister on the telephone that I was a stray, but she would take me in because her own "dear kitty, who is so very particular about whom he befriends, actually seems to like it."

That old friend of mine will not believe these notes, and so I am sending them away. I type now with a paw these final words before I return to my master in my new life.

I study. I learn.

And I warn you. Do not stand between me and any door or window I need for my escape.

Three Brothers

There once were three brothers who lived with their father in an apartment on the meanest, darkest street, in the roughest part of town in the most dangerous city in the country. One night the father said to them, "Finish your supper now. Let's get these dishes washed. Your homework? Is it all done?"

"Why?" asked the eldest brother.

"Bill is sick, and might lose his job, so I'm going out to drive his taxi tonight. You must shut the door, and lock the door, and bolt the door, and chain the door, and not open that door for anyone on Earth until I come home tomorrow."

"What if there's a fire?" asked the eldest, just to show how brave he was.

"If there is a fire, you go out the fire escape directly to a fireman who will take care of you; but don't open that door. Understand?"

All three brothers nodded their heads, "Yes, Daddy."

The three brothers watched while their father put on his warm jacket, his gloves, and his hat, checked his pocket for bus fare, and opened the apartment door.

After their father shut the door, the boys locked, bolted, and chained the door. Then they played checkers and chess, drew airplanes and made them out of paper, flew them all around the apartment. And, last of all, the eldest brother read aloud to the younger brothers until it was time for bed.

The three boys had brushed their teeth, had put on their pajamas, and turned off all the lights — except the small one in the bathroom — when a loud noise made them jump nearly out of their skins.

At the apartment door was ringing, pounding, and a voice calling out to them.

"Shhhhhhh," whispered the youngest.

"At least I can look," insisted the eldest.

"Let me see, too!" demanded the middle brother.

The eldest brother pressed his eye to the peep-hole in the apartment door. What he saw outside, what he smelled outside made him sigh with desire.

"What is it?" hissed the middle brother, pushing his big brother as hard as he could.

Punching the middle brother on the arm, the eldest brother stepped a few inches away from the door. The middle brother then pressed his eye to the tiny peephole in the door, and he, too, sighed with longing.

"Don't open it," said the smallest brother from the place where he stood watching his bigger brother. "Don't."

"Hey, guys!" called a cheerful voice from the other side of the door. "Hey. Open up. The pizza is gonna get cold. Chicken, too. And my arms are tired. Open up. It's me, your great-uncle Chester, come all this way to visit you. Yo. OPEN the door. Aren't you my great-nephews? Aren't you my men?"

Even the youngest brother, who was far from the door, could smell the hot pizza, the hot fried chicken, the sweet perfume of chocolate cake.

"Our uncle?" the eldest called through the closed door.

"Yes indeed. The brother of your grandfather, come all this way to visit you. Look at me. Look here, I'm standing the whole way back from the peephole so you can see the whole man, Uncle Chester himself! What's up? Open the door. My arms are tired."

"Don't," said the youngest brother. But nobody listened. The two elder brothers could see the man bearing a huge stack of boxes, a man wearing hand-made Italian loafers and a cashmere jacket, a man laden down with boxes. One of the boxes had words and pictures on the side the middle brother knew quite well. That box was made to contain basketball shoes, wonderful shoes touched with magic. Just to wear those shoes would make you play like a pro. Oh yes, and middle brother just knew those shoes were a gift for him, for him alone in all the world. Eldest brother? Well, he was a boy always hungry, growing tall and skinny, a bottom-less pit. The smell of good food went straight to his insides, top to toe. He longed to taste of it.

The two elder brothers unchained the door, un-bolted the door, unlocked the door, and opened the door, and brought the man bearing all those boxes inside.

The youngest brother went into their bedroom, shutting the door behind him. There he sat, on his bed, his arms hugging his knees, and listened.

The youngest brother heard the eating, the

laughing, the talking of that Uncle Chester and his two brothers. Then, bit by bit, the talking slowed down.

"So now," boomed the voice of Uncle Chester. "Who is the big guy? Who is the strong guy who will keep me company while I wait up for your daddy to come home?"

"I'll keep you company," said the eldest brother.

"Good. Good. Get out the cards. We'll cut to see who deals."

"Good night, and thanks, Great-uncle Chester," said the second brother. Yawning, he came into the bedroom, leaving the door open behind him. In his hands he carried a new pair of basketball shoes, the ones he believed had magic in them. Embracing the shoes, he lay down upon the bed and fell instantly to sleep. The youngest brother remained awake, listening.

He could hear the slap, slap, slap of cards on the table, the hearty cheerful great-uncle voice, the admiring words of his eldest brother.

"Oh no, Great-uncle Chester. You don't have to pay in real money when I win a hand. We never play for real money. I don't have real money to pay if I lose."

"Not to worry, my man. A fellow with luck like yours will never pay. I promise you."

After a time, the noise of cards, and the sounds of voices, ceased.

The apartment was silent.

In the dark, the youngest brother listened.

And he could hear a crack, crack, cracking coming from the living room.

"What is that sound?" the boy asked out loud in the dark.

"Haha. That's peanuts, my boy. I am sitting here all alone in the dark, shelling and eating peanuts." There was a great sigh, and the voice called out, "Where is the big boy? Where is the strong boy who will keep an old man company in the night?"

"I will!" The middle brother was instantly awake, leaping up from the bed, still holding the precious basketball shoes. He ran to the living room.

The youngest brother sat still in the dark, listening.

At first he saw the light in the living room go on, and he heard the slap, slap, slapping of cards on the table. He heard the laughter of that generous great-uncle voice, followed by the awed responses of his brother. "Oh, Great-uncle Chester. You don't have to pay in real money when I win a hand. We never play for real money."

"Haha. What's money for? You won, fair and

square. Now deal the cards, my man!"

After a time, the sounds of cards, the rustle of money, and the voices ceased. The light in the living room went out. The youngest brother listened in the silence.

Once again he heard a crack, crack, cracking in the night.

"What is that sound?" the boy asked out loud in the darkness.

"Ahha. It's old Uncle Chester, all alone in the night, shelling peanuts, eating peanuts, waiting."

The boy heard a great sigh, then Uncle Chester's voice saying, "And where is the big boy? Where is the strong boy who will bring an old uncle something to quench his great thirst in the night?"

At those words, the youngest brother stood up and said, "A cup of coffee is good for quenching thirst when someone is awake in the night."

"Ahhhh. There is the good boy. There is the strong boy. Bring me coffee."

"Close your eyes and open your mouth," instructed the youngest brother.

Barefoot, he padded to the kitchen. He put water on to boil. Then he took down a great, enormous mug, a joke mug that said it was the world's biggest cup of coffee. Into that mug the boy poured coffee, hot and black. As fast as he could, he carried the mug to the living room. It was so heavy that it took both hands to hold it, carefully, without spilling a drop of the steaming liquid.

There on the living-room couch sat, with eyes closed, a demon tiger with fangs as long as the boy's arms. High up near the ceiling, the nose of the demon tiger twitched, but his eyes remained closed. "Ahhh, that coffee smells GOOOODDD. See how your lazy brothers have fallen asleep?"

The third and youngest brother tore his eyes from the demon tiger's face, to where its tail softly swayed. Indeed, amidst the litter of food and gifts it was possible — though he could not see them — that his two brothers lay asleep.

Standing there in the doorway, holding the hot coffee, the youngest brother trembled. The demon tiger was so huge. How could he ever pour the coffee into that gaping mouth? As he was about to climb onto a chair, the tiger reached out with paws that were more like hands, took the mug, and drank down the coffee.

"Ahhhhhhh."

Suddenly, opening wide his two red eyes, the demon tiger roared, "But you were not fooled. You see me as I am, a demon tiger twelve thousand years old!" As he spoke, the demon tiger shrank to the size of an ordinary tiger and purred. "Ahh. You are a powerful boy. I have eaten your brothers, but you are different. You can share in my magic. You, my son, can have anything on earth you desire."

"Give back my brothers!" commanded the boy.

The tiger, which continued to shrink as they spoke, was now the size of a large housecat; he burped before replying.

"They? They are nothing. Why ask for them?"

"They are my father's riches," replied the boy.

"What? How silly. We, you and I, can give your father riches."

"No." The boy was stubborn. "My father says we three are his riches. You came as a guest into our house. You took the gift of my father's coffee from me. How can you steal from my father? Huh? How can you?"

"Oh, all right. I'll return your lousy brothers. See. Here they are." As the demon tiger spoke, the whole apartment shook. Boxes slid this way and that. On the couch, the forms of the two elder brothers took shape and became solid. The boys moved; they rubbed their eyes, stretched, and were awake.

As the boys grew solid, the tiger, the gifts, the money, and the cards — all were gone. The second brother searched everywhere for his basketball shoes, while the eldest brother sat on the couch holding his stomach, groaning. "I dreamed," he moaned, "I dreamed a demon tiger crunched my bones, and licked my flesh from his whiskers." He groaned again.

"Where?" demanded the middle brother, "Where is Great-uncle Chester? And what are you doing with that mug?"

"The man Chester is gone," said the youngest brother. "I'm taking the mug to the kitchen to wash it, and then I'm going to bed."

That Knocking
on the Wall

Tara hated these disorganized, complicated baby-sitting jobs, and wondered if she was the only one in the world who got stuck with them. She had too much homework, and was feeling way too crabby to deal with Mrs. Beale and her complicated life. Tara grumbled and kicked the leaves on the sidewalk as she approached the house, and the sitting job inside.

Mrs. Beale, breathless, hair flying as usual, babbled useless instructions and fled the scene. Tara settled down to get whatever homework she could done, while the kids were napping.

The afternoon was dark with snow to come. Maybe the kids would sleep long. Tara put on an extra sweater from her backpack. The house was cold.

She sat there with her papers as she watched the branches of a maple being pushed by the wind, back and forth, back and forth, across the dining-room window. The house was one of those old ones in a Boston suburb. It was huge, built of wood, with a brick fireplace in every room. Right now all of them were dark and cold. There were two chimneys, one at either end of the house, that went from deep in the basement, all the way up through the huge attic above the second floor. When the Beales were not going away for a month, as they were tonight, there would be fires lit in the master bedroom, living-room, and study fireplaces at least. Mrs. Beale, flaky as she was, got herself together to make those cheerful fires almost every day all winter long. Tara would have loved to sit next to one right now.

She sighed. Time to work. The kids would be up soon, and plenty to do before they went to meet Mrs. Beale, leaving the house closed up behind them.

Half an hour later, Tara realized she'd been hearing some sort of banging, not at all what the kids would make when they awoke. She put down her books, and checked the bedroom. Both of them were asleep. She went through the house, looking for windows, shutters, or rainspouts that might have come loose. Nothing. Tara stood in the hall, trying hard to find the source. It echoed so, but finally she decided that pounding came from inside the wall, near the ceiling in a spare bedroom on the second floor. Whatever made it was bigger than a squirrel, and Tara did not want to meet it.

But, then, who would? The Beales were gone ahead. The neighbors were far, beyond the huge garden, the trees and bushes and hedges. She did not even know just where they were.

The police? Maybe it wasn't that important.

The pounding continued.

Tara went back to the second-floor bedroom. "Anybody there?" she called up to the ceiling, wanting both to be heard, and not to waken the children.

No answer.

The pounding continued.

Tara called the police. The children woke up. Tara changed diapers, got them dressed, made a snack, listened to the pounding while keeping company and answering baby babble.

It was nearly time to leave; five minutes more and Tara would put on jackets and hats, and bundle the babies into their car seats. She gathered up her books.

The pounding stopped.

Tara took a big breath. Then she laughed at herself, as she realized how tensed up she'd been, listening for each blow.

A patrol car pulled into the steep driveway. Tara walked toward the door.

The pounding started up again.

Tara told the police officer about the noise, and that she had to leave, "right now," to meet the Beales in half an hour. The policeman took out a huge flashlight before he followed her into the house.

You could hear the pounding.

It was time to go.

"Is that your car on the street?" asked the officer.

"Yes."

"I'll look outside."

Tara closed the door. Time to go, but the police were outside, and the pounding inside. The babies started pulling magazines out of the rack with ripping sounds and great glee.

The police officer returned. "There's a jacket and boots on the side porch roof. Maybe your boyfriend is playing a joke."

"Certainly not." Tara did not return the policeman's grin. "I don't have that kind of boyfriend."

The policeman went up to the second floor. He crouched in each fireplace and directed his flashlight up the chimney, peering upward into the soot.

Tara, with a baby on either hip, followed the policeman downstairs.

"Stay here," he ordered when they reached the front door, then went out to his patrol car.

When he came back, he asked, "Can you reach the owners?"

"No. If I'm late, I'm sure they will call, but . . . " The babies tugged at Tara's hair, four little fists full of curls. The police officer reached over to help untangle one of them, then took the baby, who tried to get her mouth onto a shiny button.

Three squad cars, lights blazing, pulled into the drive.

"What?" Tara asked.

The police officer put down the baby on the carpet as he went to the door. Before stepping outside, he turned to Tara. "There's someone's feet, with socks and no boots — up there, in the chimney. I can't see the hands, or head, but that's who's pounding. Lucky for him, and for the fresh air of your people's house, that he won't be alone in there for a month."

This is another true story.

A Sitter and a Find

It was not a job I wanted to take. For one whole afternoon I'd be sitting with the two young Lombars at their uncle's auction house. Truth is, nobody wants to sit with those kids. At five and seven they are fifty and seventy pounds of solid, troublesome muscle: rowdy and fond of hide-and-seek, with the baby-sitter always "it."

A sitter has to keep track of them in a vast and freezing old hangar while their uncle auctions off six hours of stuff. For me the worst part was that I'd be chasing down those brats, trying to keep them from killing each other or a valued customer, or from breaking goods or themselves. In all the dashing around, often I'd catch a glimpse of something truly wonderful, something I'd love at least to look at for a good long time, even if I couldn't own it.

The seven-year-old Lombar was wheezy and

never said much, but the kid of five was loud, loud, loud! The elder, however, was sneaky, the sort that pinches and punches and pushes the little one, who then yowls so everyone thinks it's the fire department.

I got stuck with the job this time because old Mrs. Lombar cried on my mom's shoulder about how she needed just one afternoon, and she never could get one, and how desperate she was, and, and, and. My mom fell for it, and said I would. Was I mad!

Worst part was, about noon it turned dark as the inside of your pocket, so not a chance of luring the young Lombars out of doors for a good long walk. I, wearing jacket, long johns, two pairs of wool socks, gloves, boots, and a hat, and still freezing, got to the auction house about half an hour early because the papers said today the stuff for auction would be truly amazing, the whole attic of a famous toy collector.

Just inside the door, I saw dollhouses by the dozen, and sets of building blocks. They were in boxes, baskets, and some in barrels. But others stood on tables, all set up. There were cities: ancient, modern, European, Asian, Aztec, and Egyptian, each built of small painted wooden blocks, with trees, people, wooden sleds, horses, elephants, camels, sheep, cows. And on other tables were fire engines of steel, wood, and even papier-mâché.

The sale was underway, and I was looking at the stuff when Ralph, one of the cousins who works there, picked up a Gothic dollhouse and carried it out to the auction block. It was then I saw the box. It was about the size of a shoe box, wooden, painted all over in red, black, and white, with interlocking designs, the sort that have optical illusions in them. It is sort of like the things you see in a book by M.C. Escher, but this box seemed to be much, much older. With my glove, I wiped off the dust, and saw the peculiar writing on top. The words all ran together in some funny script. After staring at it for a bit, I could see that whatever it was had been written once in English: "The children's box. Always room for one more."

I tried the lid. Locked.

It seemed small for a toybox, but maybe it was made to hold a set of miniature blocks, the pieces for a game, or a set of soldiers. I shook it gently, but it made no sound. It felt empty.

Ralph came back for another dollhouse. When he saw me holding the box, he nodded toward it. "Want that?"

I shrugged. I had only about ten dollars to my name, all of it in my pocket at that minute.

"Don't clean it off like that; it draws competition. Here." He took a handful of soot from an old coal bin on the floor and dusted up the box. "Go sit down. I'll tell Pop to do it right after this dollhouse. It gives a break for the big-time dealers, so you can slip it out past them. You deserve something for yourself if you are gonna watch the monsters. Nice artwork on the sides." He winked, balanced the dollhouse on one palm, the box on the other, and walked away.

Well, yeah. I did want the box, so I went over to a chair on the side where Ralph was handing stuff up to his brother and his father, two giants nearly seven feet tall. Ralph's father is an awesome auctioneer, one who never needs a microphone.

Watching and listening, I got so caught up in the roll of the words that I nearly missed bidding. Ralph did all the work, acting as if I were bidding, so I got the box for $9.50 and had it in my hands, all wiped off by Ralph, when I set out to look for the brats.

When he handed the box to me, Ralph tried the lid, then said I should go to his mom when the auction was over, to ask her to open it for me with one of her special keys 'cause it would be a pity to break the lock. I nodded, thanked him, and then, with the box in my hands, rushed off to find the kids and their mom. I was sure I was late for the sitting job.

Yeah. I was late. Mrs. Lombar saw me coming, pointed to the boys, who were both thick with mustard as they devoured hot dogs and pretzels. As I went reluctantly toward the little Lombars, Mrs. Lombar went cheerfully out the door. When I got to the picnic bench on which the two little thugs were sitting, they abandoned their food and dashed up to me, grabbing at the box with their grubby hands.

"Whassat? Whassat?"

"Hey. Wait. Wipe your hands, and I'll show you."

"Neahhneahhhhneahhh! Wimpy box." The younger snatched it easily out of my gloved hands, and tried to bash his brother with my beautiful box.

"Careful," I whispered, hoping that I could calm him, that I could coax his mood out of the wild one into the tame. Instead he ran to the other side of a pile of sofas, with his big brother hot in pursuit. Back in a maze of passages around crates, cartons, stacks of rolled-up carpets, and furniture of all descriptions, the two boys raced, with me running close behind them. I can outrun them, but they can twist around the passages faster than I.

At one junction, the younger Lombar doubled

back, coming up behind his brother, who turned, grabbed onto the box, and started to kick his brother's legs to make him let go. I, still trying to calm them, said in the most conversational tone I could muster, "You know, it has really odd pictures on the sides, and on top there is writing that I'll bet is magic. It's in all kinds of weird languages. In English it says it is a children's box, with always room for one more."

Before I could add that we could look for their aunt, who might have a key, the lid of the box shot open. I saw the hand that reached out, grabbed one boy and then the other, and pulled them inside. Snap! The box was in my hands, with the lid locked tightly shut.

I sank down onto a moldy sofa, and I just sat there. Now what? Nobody would believe that the boys had grabbed the box, and then the box had grabbed the boys. The longer I sat, the less I could figure it out, until I got so cold that I carried the box back to where the auction was beginning to wind down.

Although I was scared to do it, I went to see Ralph's mom, and I got her to pick the lock. But, even unlocked, the lid would open only far enough for me to peek inside. Ralph's mom murmured something about putting oil on the hinges, but she was busy with the accounts, so I drifted away to the last row of chairs. I could see well enough that the box was empty.

There I sat, with the box on my lap, until I heard the high heels of Mrs. Lombar tapping on the concrete floor behind me. As I turned to face her, the lid of the box shot open, and both Lombar brats tumbled out, looking no dirtier nor more wiped out than they would have if we had spent the afternoon in the usual game of hide-and-seek. They actually said thanks for being with us before they ran off for another dose of hot dog and mustard with ketchup. Mrs. Lombar paid me, and my lovely box and I started home.

My life is set now. You have never imagined the baby-sitting I do. I can go to your house, or stay at mine. I can go to auction houses, to grocery stores, to restaurants or malls.

So, tell your mom to give me a call. There's always room for one more.

My Guardian Angel

I shuffled downstairs, half asleep. Humming to myself, eyes still mostly closed with dreaming, I crossed the hall and pushed open the kitchen door. Then, hoboy, I'm not sure whether the smell or the look of it hit me first. There, in my kitchen, all four burners of the gas stove were burning blue in the light from the window. On one of the burners, back to me, was a pointy-butt creature, sitting there in the flame, with its bare feet resting on the other burner, while it toasted marshmallows on my grandma's antique silver serving fork.

The stench was eye-melting: burning leather, charred marshmallow, singed feathers, and who knows what else? There it was, wings in the flames, smoke roiling up from the stove, a creature naked as all get out. When it turned to look at me, I could see it was purple green, with huge long ears, long face, long wings and feet and elbows, all bony. I knew I'd seen the look of it somewhere, and later I had time to think until I could remember. I had seen something like it in a picture book of cathedrals of Europe; it was a water-spout, ugly as all get out. But that first morning, hoboy, it commenced to yell at me for creating a draft.

"Well there," I said. "What are you doing in my kitchen? And why are you making such an awful mess?"

"Oh, no," says he. "This is mine. It was empty when I got here."

I said, "But I was upstairs."

"Fine." He cuts me off. "Then upstairs is yours." He hands me a greasy piece of paper, saying "Deed" on it.

Then I got all crafty and said to him, "Well then if this place is yours, then will you pay the taxes, and fix the roof, and repair the windows, and keep up the law, and do all I do?"

And he stood up there on the stove and said, "No. I'll do just what I want to do, and now I have business elsewhere, and so get out and go back upstairs."

With that he ate six flaming marshmallows from my grandma's antique silver serving fork while he put out all four burners of my gas stove by pissing on the flames.

I was yelling at him, telling him the way to turn them off, and the smell was worse than tomcat piss, and I was choking and nearly died. But then with a guardian angel there taking care of me, I couldn't; could I?

Well, I sure couldn't get any breakfast in my kitchen, so I went upstairs and got dressed. When I went out for breakfast, I met just about everyone I knew. And people were talking and talking, and I heard them, and it was everyone saying that the fellow in my kitchen was an angel, come down from heaven to take over Earth. And everyone was saying how humans have no power at all to resist the angels, and I sure agreed. Otherwise why did I do what that stinky, leathery little fellow ordered?

And later I saw all kinds of angels, some of them golden, and some silver, and some so beautiful to the eye, and some were just heads with wings, and some were wings with eyes, like to scare the daylights out of you. And the angels were everywhere, more of them coming all the time.

In no time at all, my guy (I still had trouble thinking of him as an angel, with his looks and manners and all) had given me three more nasty pieces of paper, each one saying "Deed" on it, and

with each piece of paper I was moved steadily further upstairs, until I was in the attic.

"See here!" I said to him one day when I caught
him on the staircase. "Why did you angels come
down here, anyway? I thought angels served in
heaven and were guardians to keep people out of
harm's way, and then there were bad angels. Which
ones are you?"

"That's it exactly," he said. "We are here to
guard you. Now, I need the space because more
angels are coming, so you go on up."

Now I had already explained to him that going
to the attic would be a problem. There was no
heat, no water, no way to make or store food,
nothing but dusty space, with only one tiny
window.

He hardly listened to me, but said firmly, "I will
take complete care of you. That includes food, water, comfort, everything. I am here because we angels are going to make Heaven on Earth."

I went up to the attic, and my angel did bring
me food and water, and heat, but not according to
any human time. I got cold, and sick and hungry;
hoboy did I get hungry.

"Hey. You angel. Where is some food?"

He did not answer. And there was no food.

When I went downstairs, he made me use the outside fire escape, and when I tried to tell him how things worked in the house, he said I didn't know what I was talking about. When he needed plaster, or bricks or anything for whatever it was he was doing, why he stuck his hand in the wall and just took some. I tell you my old house looked awful.

So, I was out and about on the streets a lot, and that is when I found me a beautiful, a wonderful angel, and she was so nice to me that she made me feel raptures, real raptures. She said I could come with her, and so I did, and the food was better, and the life was better, and I really thought that maybe the angels will bring it off, this Heaven on Earth; but then one day she said I did not amuse her anymore and I should just get lost.

I had to go back to my old angel, who let me back into a corner of the attic.

Today there was a parade, and the angels gave each of us a piece of paper, and told us to sing because it had arrived, Heaven on Earth. Hoboy.

New Sitter

That's all," whispered Hane. We jumped. How long had she been watching us?

In the light from the fireplace embers, the studs on her black leather jacket twinkled. "Now, off to bed, and I'll tuck you in.

"Sleep tight."

About the Author

Judith Gorog is the author of several short-story collections read and told around the world. Her work is much praised for its skillful combining of the macabre and the everyday, with touches of sly, subtle humor. Twelve more of her tales may be found in *Please Do Not Touch: A Collection of Stories*. Ms. Gorog lives in Pennsylvania with her family.

point

Other books you will enjoy, about real kids like you!

❑ MZ42599-4	**The Adventures of Ulysses** Bernard Evslin	$4.50
❑ MZ42771-7	**Blitzcat** Robert Westall	$4.50
❑ MZ43715-1	**Escape from Warsaw** Ian Serraillier	$4.99
❑ MZ40943-3	**Fallen Angels** Walter Dean Myers	$4.99
❑ MZ44479-4	**Flight #116 Is Down** Caroline B. Cooney	$4.50
❑ MZ45898-1	**The Glory Field** Walter Dean Myers	$4.99
❑ MZ44110-8	**The Greek Gods** Evslin and Hoopes	$3.99
❑ MZ43136-6	**Missing Since Monday** Ann M. Martin	$3.99
❑ MZ42792-X	**My Brother Sam Is Dead** Collier and Collier	$4.50
❑ MZ44651-7	**Sarah Bishop** Scott O'Dell	$4.50
❑ MZ42412-2	**Somewhere in the Darkness** Walter Dean Myers	$4.50
❑ MZ45680-6	**The Stranger** Caroline B. Cooney	$4.50
❑ MZ43486-1	**Sweetgrass** Jan Hudson	$3.99
❑ MZ48475-3	**Talking to Dragons** Patricia C. Wrede	$4.50
❑ MZ47478-2	**Twins** Caroline B. Cooney	$4.50
❑ MZ43412-8	**Wolf by the Ears** Ann Rinaldi	$4.99

Watch for new titles coming soon!
Available wherever you buy books, or use this order form.

Scholastic Inc., P.O. Box 7502, 2931 E. McCarty Street, Jefferson City, MO 65102

Please send me the books I have checked above. I am enclosing $_____ (please add $2.00 to cover shipping and handling. Send check or money order — no cash or C.O.Ds please.

Name_____Birthday_____

Address_____

City_____State/Zip_____

Please allow four to six weeks for delivery. Offer good in the U.S.A. only. Sorry, mail orders are not available to residents of Canada. Prices subject to change.   PNT298